For Turner,
♡

Cami Kangaroo and Wyatt Too

Cami Kangaroo

Has Too Many Sweets!

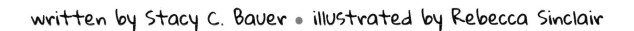

written by Stacy C. Bauer • illustrated by Rebecca Sinclair

Stacy Bauer

Cami ♡

RODNEY K
P R E S S

Cami Kangaroo Has Too Many Sweets!
Cami Kangaroo and Wyatt Too
Published by Rodney K Press
www.rodneykpress.com
info@rodneykpress.com
Minneapolis, MN

Library of Congress Control Number: 2018939250
Bauer, Stacy Author
Sinclair, Rebecca Illustrator
Cami Kangaroo Has Too Many Sweets!

ISBN: 978-0-9998141-0-9

JUVENILE FICTION

All inquiries of this book can be sent to the author.
For more information or to book an event, please visit www.stacycbauer.com

To my daughter Cami, who brings lots of
sugar (and a bit of spice)
to my life each and every day.
-S.C.B.

To my favorite dentist, my Dad.
-R.S.

All was calm in the Kangaroo house. Mommy was putting Baby Wyatt down for a nap, while Cami Kangaroo was having quiet time in her room.

At least, she was **supposed** to be having quiet time.

Instead, Cami's brain was buzzing. She could **not** stop thinking about treats.

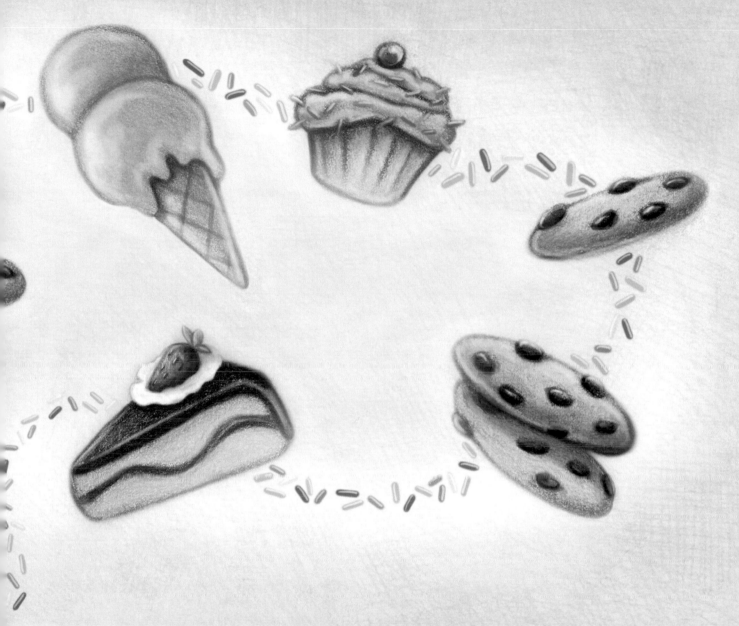

Candy, cake, cookies, ice cream...
Cami loved them all!
She knew a great place to find treats
at her house...the freezer drawer.

Cami hopped down the stairs
and over to the freezer,
grabbed the handle,
and pulled it open.

After placing the ice cream into her pouch, Cami Kangaroo hopped quickly to the playroom and locked the door behind her.

Cami Kangaroo scooped out a little of the ice cream and stuck her paws into her mouth. It was the best ice cream she had ever tasted!

She lost track of time as she tried more and more of that delicious ice cream.

"Cami?" her mommy called. Cami froze.

The playroom door rattled and slowly opened.

Mommy sighed and said, "Come here, Cami. We need to have a little talk."

"Cami, it's not okay to sneak treats," Mommy Kangaroo said.

"Treats have sugar and can cause cavities. You have a dentist appointment coming up. Next time you want a treat, you need to ask Mommy or Daddy first. Do you understand?"

Cami nodded.

But the very next day when Mommy took Wyatt upstairs for a nap,

Cami started thinking about treats again.

She quietly made her way back
to the freezer drawer.

But this time, it wouldn't open no
matter how hard she pulled.

She hopped into the pantry searching for more goodies.

The top shelf! That's where more treats were hidden!

After Mommy caught Cami
eating sprinkles in the playroom,

She removed the lock
from the playroom door
and put it on the
pantry door.

Cami still didn't give up!
She found the cupcakes
that were hidden on top
of the refrigerator
and licked off the
frosting.

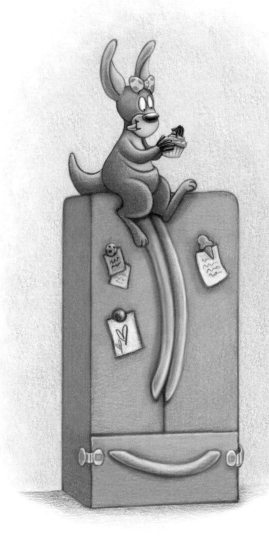

Then she ate Daddy's secret
stash of chocolate bars
that were in the drawer
next to his bed and hid the
wrappers behind her dresser.

She even found the pan of brownies Mommy hid in the microwave! Every day, Cami found **some** way to sneak a treat.

Soon after, it was time for her dentist appointment.
Cami sat in the big dentist chair.

After the hygienist cleaned and flossed her teeth, the dentist came in to take a look.

The dentist said to Mommy, "Well, I'm afraid she has four cavities."

"Cami, do you brush and floss your teeth everyday?"
Cami nodded.

"Have you been sneaking treats again?"
Mommy asked.

Cami didn't say anything. "Cami, it's very important that you listen to your parents about treats so you don't get any more cavities," said the dentist.

"I'm going to let you choose a new toothbrush and some floss.
Do you think you can stop sneaking treats?"

Cami nodded and said, "I'm sorry, Mommy."
Mommy gave her a hug.

The dentist let her pick out a new toothbrush and some floss. Then Cami and Mommy Kangaroo headed home.

When they got home, Cami bounded
quickly into the house to tell Daddy
about the dentist.

She caught him and Wyatt sitting
on the couch with a big bowl of
ice cream.

Mommy laughed. "I think it's safe to say this whole family has had **too** many sweets! It's time to change our habits- let's start with a healthy dinner."

About the Author

Born and raised in a suburb of Minneapolis, MN, Stacy C. Bauer is a wife, teacher and mother of two silly and very sweet children. She has been writing (and eating treats) since she was a child and loves sharing stories of her kids' antics and making people laugh.

To learn more about Stacy, visit her website at www.stacycbauer.com

About the Illustrator

Rebecca Sinclair has enjoyed drawing pictures since early childhood. She received her MFA in children's book illustration from the Academy of Art University in San Francisco.

You can find Rebecca illustrating in her hometown of Kalamazoo, MI with her playful french bulldog, Phoebe.

To view more of Rebecca's work, visit her website at www.rebeccasinclairstudio.com